KT-557-153

Bridgewood High FC

a new team is born

Written by Dave Spurdens

This edition published in Great Britain in 2008 by Quest, an imprint of Top That! Publishing plc,
Marine House, Tide Mill Way, Woodbridge, Suffolk, IP12 1AP, UK
www.quest-books.co.uk

0 2 4 6 8 9 7 5 3 1

Editorial Director – Daniel Graham
Creative Director – Simon Couchman
Art Editor – Matt Denny

Written by Dave Spurdens

ISBN 978-1-84666-657-5

A catalogue record for this book is available from the British Library
Printed and bound in China

Bridgewood High FC

a new team is born

Written by Dave Spurdens

Published by Quest.
Quest is an imprint of Top That! Publishing plc,
Tide Mill Way, Woodbridge, Suffolk, IP12 1AP, UK
www.quest-books.co.uk
Copyright © 2008 Top That! Publishing plc.

Follow the team online at
www.bridgewoodhighfc.com

Follow the team online and keep up to date
with the latest Bridgewood High FC action.
The fan site includes player profiles,
photographs, a player blog, league tables &
fixtures, free downloads, match reports, polls,
competitions, Bridgewood
High FC merchandise
& much more!

1

Bridgewood High opens its doors

Dermott Riley's alarm woke him at seven thirty. It was still dark and he was drenched in sweat from a vivid nightmare. He felt as though he had been chased for hours round the school playground by screaming gangs of youths all wielding sticks and knives, never being able to run fast enough to get away from them.

Getting out of bed to go to school on any day was a complete pain for 14-year-old Dermott. There couldn't be a trick he hadn't used to try to fool his mother into letting him stay at home and get out of school, all of them unsuccessful.

Today was a thousand times worse than those ordinary schooldays. This was terrifying. A new school, new surroundings, new teachers and, worst of all, a new bunch of pupils.

So many troublesome thoughts were racing through Dermott's mind. He thought he'd try it on with his mum just one more time.

'Do I have to go, Mum?' he moaned.

The sheets were pulled back and the light turned on to give the answer he knew he would get.

'You must think I was born yesterday, Dermott Riley. Going to this school is a privilege. You've seen the school. Now stop behaving like a doughnut, get yourself moving and make sure you're not late on your first day.'

It didn't help that his best friend, George Lucas, wasn't starting at the school today, even though he should have been. George's younger brother, Harry, had been injured in a hit-and-run accident, and today George was going into hospital for an operation that would hopefully give his poor brother a better quality of life.

Dermott pulled himself together at the thought of what his friend was doing. He even smacked himself round the head.

Sat on the bed, Dermott looked at himself in the mirror. It was always the same. He wished his reddish hair wasn't so wavy, and he wished he didn't have all those freckles round his eyes and nose.

Dermott stood up, stretched and yawned. 'Oh well, at least I'm not a scrawny wimp, and I'm good at football,' he mouthed at the mirror before kicking his pants against the wall.

Lots of pupils felt like Dermott: dread followed by butterflies. For others there was a sense of excitement. For Charlie Oakley there was nothing. He hadn't had time to think about it. He'd been at boxing training the evening before and by six o'clock in the morning he was on his paper round.

It didn't matter much to Charlie. He was a lucky kid. Whatever was placed in front of him in life he would work his way through it – solidly, comfortably, with a smile and determination.

His grandad had always told him that the most important thing in life was to deal with things. Charlie had listened.

Bridgewood High School had taken three years to build, and soon hundreds of pupils would join Dermott and Charlie and swarm through its high chrome and glass doors for the first time. It was an impressive building and had won an award for 'Best Modern Design in East London'.

The image of Albinus Gardiner sauntering towards the entrance of the school did not suggest he had any great hopes for Bridgewood High. The knot of his school tie hung a foot away from his shirt collar, his shirt fluttered outside his trousers and his hair looked as though it had been in a fight with the comb.

In complete contrast, Albinus's friend from his previous school, Sam Smith, strolled by his side and looked as though he was modelling the school uniform for a clothes catalogue.

Regardless of how they both looked, their minds were occupied by the same thought: getting to the sports hall, with its superb gymnasium and indoor football pitch.

They weren't alone in that thought. Most of the pupils who were mad keen on sport knew they were lucky to be going to Bridgewood High. No other school in the area had the same facilities.

The headmaster, Mr Hyde, had decided he wanted the students to use their first day to get to know their new school and meet the teaching staff. His only stipulation was that by home time they had been to see every teacher in the school.

It was no coincidence that the first place all the sporting pupils made for was the sports hall.

The first person they met was Mr Grant, the head of physical education. They were introduced to his deputy, Mr Cauldwell, and Miss Cranson, who took most of the girls' sports subjects.

Mr Cauldwell was the football man. He was an ex-professional who still played in the Conference League. Most of the students were surprised to find out that Miss Cranson would also take football coaching. 'How could such a beautiful woman with a figure that good, even in a tracksuit, know anything about football?' was the thought racing through the minds of many of the teenage boys. In time they would learn that Miss Cranson played for a famous women's football team and might be picked, soon, to play for England.

Mr Grant had to remind the students in the sports hall that they could not stay there all day, and that there was more to Bridgewood High than just playing sport.

Even though they had to move on, the lads' main topic of conversation was football – who they supported and why.

They soon learned that their favourite teams weren't just in London; they were all over the country. Dougie Butt, whose family were from Scotland, supported Celtic; Johnny Cunningham, who had gone to school in Tyneside, supported Newcastle. Salam Chalabi was born in Iraq, but supported Chelsea because his uncles were season ticket holders.

Salam felt as though he had won a scholarship getting into Bridgewood High. His life had not been easy. He came to England when he was nine, after his father, having fought in the Gulf War, was reported missing, presumed dead. Life in Iraq had been very hard for Salam's mother after the disappearance of her husband.

Salam dreamt that one day his father would turn up at their house in England. His mother would rather he did not harbour this dream, believing it made him sad. But Salam argued that it made him happy, adding, 'One day it will happen, you just wait and see.'

These three boys were joined by Christopher Coggins, a small lad who walked with a limp.

Christopher was born with a serious hip defect and had been in and out of hospital for operations to remedy the condition. The nurses and doctors christened him 'Miracle Boy' when he recovered, especially when he was picked for his junior school's football team.

Christopher supported Millwall because he thought Millwall was in the East End of London, where he lived. By the time he found out they were in South London, it was too late. He was a big fan.

Many of the boys who had met up in the sports hall found themselves going to other departments together, talking heatedly about football. Wandering aimlessly, a few of them found themselves in the art and graphic design studios.

Johnny Cunningham liked art because he thought it was easy. 'Art's always a good skive. Splash a bit of paint, cut up some paper, that sort of thing. Doesn't tax the brain, does it?'

Dougie Butt echoed this sentiment, but Salam was looking at the pictures that hung on the walls with a more serious expression. He liked art, especially drawing portraits. He tried to explain this to his new school friends.

'I don't remember my dad too well. I was really young when he disappeared while fighting in the Gulf War. Mum and I left Iraq shortly after he vanished. The only photo I have of him was taken on his wedding day, and I've used it to draw loads of pictures of him since. Mum says she's shocked at how alike him my sketches look. I just know that when he comes back I'll recognise him.'

'So you reckon he's still alive?' Johnny Cunningham asked in his broad Geordie accent.

'I know he is. One day ...'

Dermott Riley and Jack Mayhew left the sports hall together and decided they would wander down to the drama and dance studios. They talked about their friend George Lucas and wondered how he had got on with his operation.

George was having part of his liver removed, which would then be grafted onto his brother's liver. It was a brave thing to do. If the surgery worked, his brother's quality of life should improve dramatically.

'I'll never eat liver again,' quipped Dermott. 'Ugh. Mum and Dad love it. Liver and bacon. Hearts, too. Sheep hearts and pigs' hearts. I've told her: "Don't serve that stuff for my tea." Can you imagine? They tell me it's "offal". I say dead right, it's awful. Get it Jack? Offal, awful. Play on words, Jack!'

Dermott never stopped joking. He remembered every joke he'd ever been told and had a quip for any occasion. He loved Irish jokes especially, and always told them in an authentic accent.

Usually Jack loved Dermott's jokes, but Dermott could tell that, today, something was up. Jack obviously had something on his mind. Maybe he'd get round to telling Dermott when the time was right for him.

At least Dermott felt okay now – a lot better than when he woke up first thing that morning. Fancy thinking the students would be chasing him round the playground with sticks and knives. What was that word his mum had called him? A doughnut. He decided he liked that word and he thought he might just like this school.

2

Different school,
same problems

The next morning, coming into school, Jimmy Cork saw his old friend Jack Mayhew scuffing his feet against the kerb and looking miserable.

'Cheer up, Jack, it may never happen!'

'It already has, Jimmy,' Jack returned mournfully. 'I've just seen Pollard and Chapman, those two bullies from our old school.'

'So what? You're older and bigger now. Don't let them worry you.'

'They're older too, Jimmy. And they look a lot bigger than me.'

Jimmy cast a glance at Jack. He was right there. The word 'scrawny' sprang immediately to mind. It was amazing that Jack was so good at football. His face was drawn, his arms were frail, and his legs were the skinniest Jimmy had ever seen on a football pitch.

'What makes you think they'll carry on the bullying? They'll get thrown out of this school if they start that again,' said Jimmy.

'They've started already. Yesterday Matthew Chapman shook his fist at me and Dan Pollard ran his hand across his throat. Today they were sneering at me as I came through the school gates – and I don't think they were trying to be friendly, do you?'

'Report them to the Head, then. Don't let it go on. Dob 'em in.'

'And if I do, what happens next? I'd have their brothers ganging up on me and even Chapman's dad. He's a right bully.'

'Well, your dad's big. Let him go round and sort it out.'

'My dad's big, but he's not a fighter. He's a peaceful man. He plays chess and likes going fishing. Chapman's dad's a thug and he's been to prison for it. He stabs people!'

Jimmy Cork could sympathise with Jack, in a funny kind of way. Jimmy was known by a lot of people in the East End of London because of his family history. His father and many of his uncles had a reputation for their exploits on the wrong side of the law. By the time Jimmy went to junior school his mother had tried her hardest to give the family an air of respectability – which hadn't been easy because Jimmy's father was serving a twenty-five-year prison sentence.

Jimmy found it tiresome that everybody he met wanted to talk about his family's dubious past. He wanted the same as his mother: for the family to change and separate itself from their history. Jimmy intended to get a good education and make his way in life on the right side of the law.

The trouble was, things kept cropping up – like wanting to help Jack put a stop to the bullying.

Meanwhile, the crowd gathered round the sports hall noticeboard suggested that some important announcements had been posted.

Jimmy pushed his way to the front of the crowd so that he could read the notice.

He studied the message and was interested to learn that a school house system was to be introduced. The notice stated that pupils would be selected for one of the four houses: Yellow, Blue, Red and Green.

All in-school competitions would be between houses, and the first was a 5-a-side football tournament which would kick off next week. Mr Grant had called a meeting of all those players who wanted to take part.

In the meantime, Key Stage 4 pupils were invited to visit the teaching areas for subjects that were not part of the compulsory curriculum.

Timothy Houghton-Smith had been thrilled by the sports facilities that he had seen on the first day, but found himself just as excited when he went to the music studios. Equipped with a vast array of instruments and recording equipment, there was also a piano identical to the one his mother had at home.

Miss Green, the music teacher, had been waiting for Timothy's visit. She had seen from his report that he played guitar and piano.

There weren't many people opting for music, but Timothy recognised Angelo Paggio from the sports hall the day before.

'Hey, Paggio! Voice of an angel, eh?' Timothy laughed at his own joke.

'Heh, some might say so! Well, before my voice broke, anyway. Got me roped into the choir at St Paul's Cathedral. Are you the musical type, too?'

Timothy's route to Bridgewood High had taken a curious mix of twists and turns. Up to the age of fourteen he had attended a very expensive boarding school in Cheshire. Unfortunately, the family firm had fallen on hard times and the Houghton-Smiths found themselves living a new life in Essex. Surprisingly, Timothy was unaffected by the family fall.

'Yes, well, I want to be in a band at some point. This place has a better music room than my old school! Mind you, it's better in lots of ways – at least they play football here, not rugby,' Timothy enthused.

Timothy loved football. He had practised a lot with his grandad, who used to play for the army. Timothy loved the game so much he used to sneak out of his posh school to play for the local village team. Timothy hated the fact that his old school only played rugby and hockey.

Football and music weren't the only things Timothy was good at. He was outstanding at foreign languages and, unlike most schoolchildren, loved maths. He also excelled at English and drama, and could write fluently on a lot of different subjects.

It meant that Timothy was always in great demand at the last school he attended, and it would be the same at Bridgewood High – not only from the students but the teachers as well.

The demand had already begun in Mr Newlove's English class. Mr Newlove wanted to start a school magazine straight away and he prided himself on being a very good judge of character. None of the pupils at Bridgewood High came without a history, and there were files on each pupil showing their progress at their previous schools.

Mr Newlove had found Timothy's file particularly interesting. He saw straight away that if there was one pupil capable of being the editor of the school magazine, it was Timothy.

When Mr Newlove announced his support for Timothy's editorship, Timothy sat back in his chair and thought 'here we go again'. He knew from that moment on he would have little time to himself.

Timothy's fate was sealed when the whole class voted unanimously for him to be editor.

The day had flown by, and it was time to go to the 5-a-side meeting in the sports hall. Now that the house teams had been decided, there was an air of excitement and a lot of conversation about who would be playing with whom. Many of the boys had already made each other's acquaintance, and were looking forward to playing against one another in the tournament. The staff had high hopes, too, with so many players taking part. Surely they must be able to pick a decent school team?

The PE staff took charge of three of the houses. Mr Grant became manager of Yellow House, Mr Cauldwell drew Blue House, and Miss Cranson would manage Green House. The Headmaster, Mr Hyde, was such a keen football fan, he took the manager's job for Red House. Due to the great level of interest in the competition, each house fielded an 'A' and a 'B' team.

Mr Grant decided he would select the teams by drawing the players' names out of a hat. It looked good for Yellow House 'A' when the talents of Albinus Gardiner, Duc Duong and Dougie Butt were drawn in the same team.

The students were delighted that the draw was being made there and then, and a date was set for the first matches. Yellow 'A' would kick off the tournament against Blue 'A'. The Blue 'A' team also looked like a strong side and would benefit from the talents of Dicky Woodward, Luan Havolli and Jack Mayhew. The opening match promised to be a scorcher.

There was only one glum face in the crowd when the date for the first group games was announced. Jimmy Cork could not believe his bad luck. He would be going to visit his dad in prison that day. There would be no getting out of it, either. The one thing his mum insisted on was that Jimmy went to see his father in prison.

'Every time I go, Jimmy, you go. I don't want you ever thinking there's anything glamorous about being in prison. There's people round here who think it's a badge of honour. Well, it's not, and I want you to see that it isn't.'

Jimmy could hear her voice if he asked to be excused. The trouble was, he had no intention of following in his father's footsteps. Seeing his father come into the prison visitor centre, with a yellow sash across his shirt and a warder taking him to his seat, made his stomach turn over.

In contrast, Jack Mayhew was feeling much happier and had decided that he was going to stand up to his tormenters. Jimmy's support had made him stronger and Jack had taken on a defiant attitude.

At the 5-a-side meeting, Jack stood and chatted to Dicky Woodward. He learned that Dicky's family had moved to East London from where Jack's family used to live. It turned out that Jack's mum and Dicky's dad had gone to the same school. In a funny way, the coincidence made Jack feel even stronger.

It was while they were exclaiming about this coincidence that Jack caught sight of the two people he did not want to see. Matthew Chapman and Dan Pollard had strolled into the sports hall and were standing by the entrance, pointing at him.

'See those two over by the entrance there? D'you know them?' Jack asked Dicky.

'No, but when I was over at the IT centre, they asked me if I knew where you lived now,' Dicky replied. 'Why are they interested in you, anyway?'

'They were at my last school – they were the school bullies. Used to nick people's bikes and flog 'em, and rob kids of their dinner money, all that sort of thing.'

'Big geezers, ain't they? I suppose that's why they get away with bullying. Stay away from 'em, Jack. They look trouble to me,' Dicky warned.

'They're hard to stay away from, Dicky.

You're not hard to find in a school, are you?
I can't make out why they want to make my life
a misery. I don't like the idea of them trying to
find out where I live.'

At that moment Charlie Oakley came over to
join them. A pretty girl was by his side.

'Those two kids over by the door, d'you two
know who they are?' he asked, putting his arm
around the girl's shoulders.

'Unfortunately, I do,' Jack volunteered.
'Trouble with a capital T. They used to go to my
old school. They were the school bullies. Why do
you ask?'

'They were giving my girlfriend, Mitzi – by the
way, this is Mitzi – a lot of hassle over at the IT
centre. She was quite upset.'

Jack and Dicky couldn't take their eyes off
Mitzi. Charlie smiled. He was used to other boys
looking at his girlfriend like that. She was
exceptionally beautiful with long, wavy brown
hair and dreamy hazel eyes.

Jack described to Charlie some of the awful things the bullies had done at his old school, and all the time Charlie kept his eye on them. Eventually, he and Mitzi moved off towards where Pollard and Chapman were standing. Before Charlie got to the doors, the bullies had disappeared from sight.

Strange goings on
at the 5-a-side

As Jimmy Cork's mum headed for the prison, Jimmy sat glumly in the passenger seat.

He couldn't stop thinking about the start of the 5-a-side tournament. He knew how hard it was for his mother to see her husband in those conditions, but that didn't make the leaden feeling in his guts go away.

The day could have started better for Dicky Woodward, too. His parents had a blazing row and his father stormed out of the house, saying he wasn't coming back. Dicky thought the world of both his parents and the notion of his father going off and never being seen again sent a shiver down his spine.

Dicky had known for a while that his parents were not getting on well, and this morning he had heard his mother accuse his dad of having an affair.

On the bus to school, Dicky couldn't stop thinking about what his mum had said. He couldn't imagine his dad, who always seemed so solid and reliable, having an affair. He tried convincing himself that his mum had accused his dad in blind anger but, try as he did, he couldn't get the nagging doubts to go away.

Dicky was a pedigree East Ender. As a young child, his parents and grandparents had groomed him to work on the family market stall in Petticoat Lane. He enjoyed working there because of the people he worked with. He liked their sense of humour and the way they all stuck together. Dicky had the same sense of humour. He loved the wisecracks – the snappy jokes and the leg pulling. He was known to be a bit of a practical joker himself. No one's shoelaces were safe when Dicky was around!

For most of the students involved in the

5-a-side tournament, it was hard to think about anything but the football that afternoon – but there were some lessons to be negotiated first.

Timothy Houghton-Smith, Dermott Riley and Dicky Woodward were about to become acquainted with the unusual teaching methods of Mr Newlove.

Dermott Riley made the mistake of revealing his non-academic side to Mr Newlove, and had the shock of his life when he was caught gazing out of the window. Mr Newlove launched the marker pen lid that he held in his hand across the room with pinpoint accuracy, and it pinged off the side of Dermott's head.

To Dermott's dismay, the entire class dissolved into laughter. When the lesson finished, Dicky Woodward found it hard to control his mirth. 'You should have seen your face when the pen lid connected,' he told Dermott. Dermott mumbled something about the teacher being out of order by way of a sheepish reply.

'Bet you don't do it again, mate,' Dicky observed, with a mischievous grin on his face, as they moved off down the corridor.

The general consensus of the pupils was that they liked Mr Newlove and enjoyed his first lesson. Most of the girls thought he was quite handsome, and they liked his cheeky smile. One of the girls, Hannah Jardine, thought he looked like a spitfire pilot from World War II, with his big, bushy moustache. Lauren Gooch liked his laughing blue eyes and thought that when he was younger, he probably looked like Timothy Houghton-Smith. Timothy hadn't taken his eyes off Lauren since they entered the classroom and was secretly quite pleased by her declaration.

There was a happy buzz about the throng as they moved off to a history lesson with Mr Bisheno. Hannah and Lauren both hoped it would be on World War II and spitfires.

'You've got it bad, you two!' laughed Dicky Woodward.

'Yeah – hands up who loves Mr Newlove!' teased Dermott. 'Mind you, he's definitely old enough to have been in World War II.' Dermott wasn't going to forget his humiliation at the hands of Mr Newlove just yet.

Albinus Gardiner, Duc Duong and Sam Smith were about to experience the equally unusual teaching practice of Mr Reece in the school's richly equipped science suite.

Mr Reece had decided to commence his classes with a biology lesson. Today's topic was 'The form and arrangement of the parts of the human body'. That was until the class filed in and took their seats.

Albinus Gardiner looked around at the work benches, with their gas taps and racks of glass test tubes. He fought to suppress a groan, but could not hold back a yawn.

'Albinus, do you know why you yawned just now?' asked Mr Reece, his large red face beaming a questioning expression.

'Boredom, Sir?'

It was the cue for Mr Reece to improvise. The lesson would now be about the science of yawning, and turned out to be interesting enough to hold the attention of Albinus and the rest of the class.

As they all filed out, the class agreed that Mr Reece was a good, if unorthodox, teacher and that the lesson was one of the best science classes they had ever been to.

Meanwhile, as the final bell of the day concluded its last chime, Jack Mayhew neared the entrance to the sports hall. George Lucas's mum had just phoned to let him know that George was alright and that the operation on young Harry had gone well. She told him he could visit George in hospital that same evening if he wanted to. It was great news, and Jack couldn't wait to tell Dermott. Jack was sure that Dermott would want to go with him.

As the players began to file into the dressing room to get changed for the 5-a-side tournament, Jack told them all the good news about George and Harry. Many of the boys knew George from their previous schools or had heard what a good footballer he was.

Yellow 'A' and Blue 'A' were the first teams to run onto the pitch. There could not have been a more rip-roaring match to get the tournament under way. It ended 5–4 to the Yellows.

Standout players included Albinus Gardiner and Duc Duong, who scored two goals each for the Yellows, while Luan Havolli and Dicky Woodward scored a goal apiece for the Blues.

Everybody was impressed with Duc Duong's performance. He was very fast and tricky to tackle, and worked well with Albinus. They were friends from junior school and lived in the same street.

Mr Grant was delighted with his team's performance, and Mr Cauldwell was not unhappy with the way Blue House had performed, despite going down to a narrow one-goal defeat. He was very pleased with his whole team, but Dicky Woodward stood out as an exceptional talent and demonstrated why he enjoyed the nickname 'Tricky Dicky', with a selection of skills on the ball that had some of his opponents chasing shadows.

At the end of the group games, the way was clear to draw the knockout semi-final matches. Yellow 'A' would play Red 'B' and Blue 'A' would play Green 'B'.

Mr Cauldwell was delighted that many of the players who had stood out in the preliminary games would be involved in the semis. He was thinking ahead to when trials would be held for the school first and second elevens, and the 5-a-sides had given him a real idea of who would be involved.

The semis and the final would be played after school the following afternoon. Mr Grant was sure that a lot of students would like to watch the games.

As the players trooped off to the dressing rooms, the PE staff came together in Mr Grant's office to discuss the players that had impressed them the most.

Mr Cauldwell wrote up three headings on a whiteboard: Definites – Probables – Possibles.

'That's how I see it after watching those games. Let me know what you think to my choices.'

He had started writing the name of Charlie Oakley when there was a commotion outside the room. Mr Cauldwell looked up and saw Hamit Erbakan burst out of the changing rooms, throwing his arms in the air and shouting 'My stuff's gone! Someone's robbed me. There's a pickpocket!'

Mr Grant soon had the door open and was asking Hamit to calm down.

'Somebody's rifled my pockets,' said Hamit. 'My bus fare, my watch and my key – they've gone!'

Mr Grant showed Hamit to a chair. 'Now, you're sure you had those things in your pockets when you got changed?'

'Certain. I had the exact fare, my watch that my mum bought me for my birthday, and the front door key on a keyring.'

In no time at all Mr Hyde had arrived at the sports hall. Mr Cauldwell had taken charge and had got everybody involved in the 5-a-side tournament lined up for a search. Three boys had turned out their belongings when there was a shout from the rear of the queue.

'I've got them, Sir! In my pocket. Those things you just said. They're in my pocket, but I never put them there. I've got no idea how they got in my pocket – I swear,' pleaded Jack Mayhew.

The whole queue swivelled round to catch sight of an ashen-faced Jack moving towards Mr Cauldwell with the keyring, some money and a watch in his hand. He was bent over and peering incredulously at his hands, his face creased in anguish. He was murmuring, 'I didn't take them. It wasn't me. It wasn't me.'

Mr Grant moved towards Jack and took the items. Mr Hyde told the rest of the pupils to wait in the sports hall until further notice.

Mr Hyde placed his arm around Jack's shoulders and ushered him into the office. Hamit remained seated and looked flabbergasted. Mr Cauldwell handed him back his possessions.

'Innocent until proven guilty; that's how I propose to handle this matter. Hamit, you have your valuables back and, on the face of it, Jack Mayhew was in possession of them. There will be a thorough investigation into this, and only when that has been concluded will the blame be apportioned.'

Mr Cauldwell indicated for Jack Mayhew to sit down. 'Now, Jack, how do you think Hamit's possessions came to be in your pocket?'

'I don't know, Sir. I don't know,' Jack tearfully

replied. His voice quivered and he was shaking all over.

'Tell me your movements from when you went to the changing rooms and during the 5-a-side games.'

'I just took my sports bag in there, and found a seat and a peg to hang my clothes, got changed and came out onto the pitch ready to play. I never went back until after the last match when most of the other players were already back there getting showered or changed.'

'And that was it? You didn't go there in between, when there would have been nobody else about?'

'Never. I never left the games. I watched every match,' Jack replied solemnly.

'Okay. When you watched the teams playing, who did you stand with? Did you talk to anybody? Is there anybody who would know if you left pitchside?'

'I was with Dicky Woodward and Luan

Havolli before we played our game, and after that it was just Dicky. Luan was with Sam Smith but close to us. He would have seen me all the time.'

Mr Grant called Dicky Woodward and Luan Havolli into the office to corroborate Jack's account of his whereabouts.

To Jack's utter relief, Dicky and Luan both confirmed his sequence of events. Both boys were absolutely sure Jack had never left the sports hall.

Suddenly, Hamit stood up from his chair and pointed to Jack.

'I don't think Jack did it, Sir – and I don't want him blamed. I haven't known him for long but he's not the type to steal. I can see that. I don't know how it happened but I know it wasn't Jack.'

The teachers agreed that Jack should carry on playing in the tournament until the matter was resolved.

Mr Hyde addressed the pupils waiting in the sports hall and told them that they were free to go home. 'And I don't want you saying anything about what happened this afternoon. There will be a proper investigation, but in the meantime I do not want the rest of the school gossiping about this incident. Off you go, then,' Mr Hyde said sternly.

As Dicky, Luan and Hamit left the sports hall, they assured Jack that they knew he could not have been the thief.

The bullies learn a lesson

The pressures on Jack Mayhew as he entered
Bridgewood High the next day were enormous.
It mattered very little that Mr Hyde had sworn
everybody to silence over the incident. It was the
talk of the school.

As Jack came through the school gates, he saw
a group of boys whispering and gesturing
towards him. No matter how hard he tried, Jack
could not escape the fact that he felt like going
into hiding.

'My God,' he thought, 'is this what it's going
to be like from now on?' Jack had come to
Bridgewood High full of expectations, but now,
within a few days, the school seemed to cling
around him like a suffocating ghost. How would
he ever stop his fellow pupils from whispering
and suggesting that he was a thief?

Jack hadn't told his mum and dad about the incident. His dad would go mad. 'Honesty is the best policy,' was one of his dad's favourite phrases. He would hardly welcome the news that, in his first week at a new school, his son was looked upon as a petty criminal.

At that moment, Dicky, Hamit and Luan edged alongside Jack and his taut muscles started to relax.

'Hold your head up, Jack, and get a grip. Pull your shoulders back. Don't act like a guilty man. We'll sort this out between us – honest. We're on your side.' Dicky's voice gave Jack hope, and he felt for a moment that he could fight back and clear his name.

They sauntered into school to be greeted by Charlie Oakley and Mitzi Hasset. Charlie spoke directly to Jack. 'You've been fitted up, mate, and I might know who did it ...'

Jack goggled at him, finding it hard to believe what he was hearing. Then Mitzi spoke.

'Yeah – I saw Pollard go to the changing rooms while the games were going on. He looked well shifty. I think he's as scared of Chapman as everybody else, you know.'

'Hey, I'm not scared of either of them! All bullies are cowards,' Charlie protested.

Jack brightened up. His frown disappeared and, for the first time since he had been labelled a thief, a smile spread across his face.

The fact that he was still being allowed to play in the tournament hadn't quite sunk in with Jack. He was convinced that as soon as the items had been discovered in his possession he would have been banned from taking any further part, but the staff were adamant that no such thing was going to happen.

Even the dread of his father finding out what had happened was fading and, as Jack made his way to his seat, he felt better than he had done since he first clapped eyes on his tormentors at Bridgewood High.

Jack had been to visit George Lucas in hospital the night before, and seeing his friend so unexpectedly bright had lifted his spirits. According to the doctors, the graft had taken and Harry was making good progress. George was sad that he couldn't take part in the 5-a-side tournament, but the thought of his brother having a better life was more important to him at this stage.

Most of the boys due to play in the semi-finals found it hard to concentrate on their lessons, and it was almost impossible for Jack to do so after everything that had happened. If it wasn't the thought of Pollard and Chapman going to such extreme lengths to fit him up as a thief, then it was the thought that he was playing in such an exciting tournament with his newfound friends.

Albinus Gardiner could not concentrate on lessons at the best of times, but trying to disguise his complete lack of interest in his first technology lesson with Mr Pidgeon tested every sinew in his body. By the time the lesson was halfway through he had scored three glorious, imaginary goals and his team had thrashed the Red House 'B' team 10–0.

The announcement by Mr Pidgeon that 'there endeth the first lesson' had Albinus mouthing 'Yes, yes, yes!' at the ceiling, and floating down the corridor with only one more lesson to go before kick-off.

Meanwhile, there was good news for Jimmy Cork, who had missed the opening games because of a visit to see his father in prison. A player in Green's 'B' team had twisted an ankle and Miss Cranson wanted Jimmy to play in his place. Miss Cranson had heard good reports about Jimmy's footballing ability from his last school and from other players in the tournament – he was a natural choice to replace the injured lad.

Jimmy was in doubly high spirits. He had just

been told about a possible appeal that could see his father being released from prison early. He wasn't sure whether it was the prospect of having his dad at home again or the thought of not having to make those awful visits any more that filled him with such joy. Jimmy's conscience told him that it was probably a bit of both.

It wasn't long after the last afternoon lesson that the sports hall began to fill up with players and spectators, and a buzz of expectancy hung high in the rafters of that impressive building.

Mr Grant, Mr Cauldwell, Miss Cranson and Mr Hyde were all in the PE office and could be seen having a lively discussion that, no doubt, included some speculation about the forthcoming results of the tournament.

Mr Reece should have refereed the first match, but had been replaced by Mr Mansell. Mr Mansell was Miss Cranson's boyfriend and had applied for the part-time job of Football

Development Officer at Bridgewood High. That
such a position was available showed how
seriously the headmaster regarded football at
the school.

Charlie Oakley wasn't at all surprised that
Mr Reece had stood down as referee this time.
Earlier in the day, Mitzi had told Mr Reece
that she thought Jack had been set up by
Matthew Chapman and Dan Pollard. Mr Reece
believed Mitzi.

In twenty years of teaching, Mr Reece had
encountered a lot of bullies like Pollard and
Chapman and he was concerned. He feared that
the two bullies would not let the matter rest once
they learned that Jack was still playing in the
tournament. He offered to help Mitzi prove
Jack's innocence.

As the spectators began to take their seats, the
buzz that had earlier been a drone was now
rising to a level of noisy excitement.

When Charlie Oakley led Yellow 'A' onto the

pitch, he was pleased to see that Mitzi was sitting in the crowd with a restrained smile on her face. Matthew Chapman and Dan Pollard had taken their places one row in front of where she was sitting.

As expected, the first semi-final went off at breakneck speed, but with a lot of accurate passing and good movement. A slick one-touch move between Duc Duong and Albinus Gardiner ended in a fierce shot past the Reds' keeper, allowing Yellow House to take an early lead.

The surprise package for Red House was Timothy Houghton-Smith. For a tall lad, his control on the ground surprised Mr Hyde, and his ability to keep the ball, despite frantic efforts to take it away from him, prompted the headmaster to offer comparisons between the way Timothy played with the way Italian players screened and kept the ball.

The semi-finals were seven minutes each way with a one minute break at half-time.

Six minutes into the first half and Angelo Paggio rammed home a scorching goal for Red House. He beat one player with a cheeky drag-back and went past another by feigning to shoot, before slotting the ball home past a helpless keeper.

During the half-time break, Charlie Oakley noticed that Dan Pollard was not in his seat and that Matthew Chapman seemed to be looking around anxiously. Charlie glanced at Mitzi, who had a mischievous grin on her face and gave Charlie the thumbs-up sign when she saw he was looking her way.

Then it was game on for the second half. Hamit Erbakan showed what a good reader of the game he was, having correctly identified that Duc Duong was the Yellow House supply line. He marked him tightly, and the fluid play Yellows had shown in the first half dried up – until Albinus took a threaded pass from Charlie on his thigh and volleyed the ball into the net.

Yellow House withstood a barrage of pressure from Hamit, Angelo and Timothy, but managed to hold out to the final whistle. They were through to the final, and in the next fifteen minutes they would know which team they would battle in the climax of the competition.

Charlie Oakley was looking for somewhere to sit to watch the game between Blue House and Green House when he saw Mr Reece come out of the changing room, carrying what looked like a camera bag over his shoulder. When Charlie noticed that Dan Pollard was back in his seat, he felt a twinge of disappointment that the bully was not being frog-marched out of the hall with his arm bent up his back.

Blues won the toss in the next semi-final and swept straight up the pitch from the kick-off in a three-pass move to put the ball in the back of the net. Jack Mayhew was mobbed by the rest of his team for what had been a great goal.

Above the commotion of the game, Jack

could hear a shrill, high pitched whistle coming from the spectators. He looked up to see Mitzi Hasset with two fingers in her mouth, jumping up and down. It seemed strange to see such a pretty, elegant girl doing such a thing. He noticed Pollard and Chapman sitting in front of her, unmoved.

As they were about to restart, Jack looked up again to see Mitzi give him the thumbs-up sign. Jack wasn't sure whether it was for the quality of the goal he had just scored or if something else had happened.

If it hadn't been for Peter Schirtzer's sterling performance in goal for Green House, the Blues would have turned round at half-time at least four goals up. As it was, the Greens started the second half just one goal behind and took the game to the Blues right from the kick-off.

Four minutes into the second half and Aaron Jacobs went on a solo run, beat two players and blasted a scorching drive past the keeper to level the scores. Blue House was the bigger, stronger side, and were it not for the hard tackling of Jimmy Cork and intelligent passing of Salam Chalabi, they could have run away with it. The Greens dug in valiantly, but they were unable to stop Jack Mayhew as he went on another of his mazy runs to stab in a second goal.

Mitzi Hassett's constant whistling and her unbridled enthusiasm had spread along the seats on both sides of her. Everybody was on their feet and cheering, except Pollard and Chapman. Unlike their last encounter, when they had been rude to Mitzi, Pollard and Chapman now appeared to be ignoring her. It seemed the bullies' behaviour had changed now they knew she was Charlie Oakley's girlfriend.

The final was between Yellow House 'A' and Blue House 'A', with everybody who had played in the semi-finals giving a good account of themselves and impressing Mr Grant and Mr Cauldwell massively.

'How can there be so many good players in one school?' beamed Mr Grant. 'It's truly remarkable.'

The rest period between the semis and the final would be fifteen minutes, during which time all the PE staff and Mr Hyde filed into the office. Minutes later, Mr Reece arrived with Mitzi and what looked like a very intense meeting was soon under way.

Meanwhile, all the players were sitting together. Charlie Oakley turned to Jack Mayhew and whispered, 'All happening in there, Jack – and I don't think they're talking about the football, do you?'

'Don't know, Charlie – what do you think they're talking about, then?'

'Come on, Jack. They're talking about you. Why would Mitzi be in there if they were talking about the football?'

'Talking about me? Those goals weren't that good!' laughed Jack.

'You're winding me up! You must know what's going on? You wait …'

Mr Mansell called the finalists over for a warm up session as they had been sitting around for a long while.

Albinus Gardiner made sure he had taken up a position in the middle of the group, where he could not be seen by Mr Mansell, and went through the motions of stretching. Each movement was accompanied by a giant yawn, with a few break-dancing moves thrown in for humorous effect. By the time the exercises were finished, Duc Duong and Dicky Woodward were holding their sides trying to contain their laughter.

Blues won the toss and kicked off. They had listened to Mr Cauldwell's advice not to give the ball away cheaply. After ten consecutive passes, Yellows finally had a touch of the ball. It was a devastating touch as Albinus Gardiner robbed Dicky Woodward, passed to Dougie Butt, and the big striker smashed the ball into the back of the net.

Blue House were stunned. Mr Cauldwell was jumping around and shouting for his team to keep their chins up and carry on the way they were playing.

It paid off. Jack Mayhew and Luan Havolli worked two give-and-go triangles before Luan slotted a clever side-foot shot into the net. Mr Cauldwell could not contain his delight – not just because they had scored, but because of the quality of the move. All the team managers applauded the show of skill, which had set the final on a knife edge.

Mr Hyde's face shone with appreciation as he turned to Mr Grant and slapped him on the back, 'I don't know about you, and it is early days, but I think we have something special going on here. I feel like a panhandler who has just struck gold.'

'Don't get carried away, Sir – as you said, it's

early days; but I do know what you mean. By the way, what's a panhandler?' Mr Grant cheekily replied.

The first half ended with both sides level, and the next seven minutes promised to produce a humdinger.

Three minutes were allowed for a half-time break, and both teams went into a huddle to talk tactics and fire each other up. Mr Cauldwell relayed the same message as the first half. 'Keep it tight at the back, lads – and don't give the ball away cheaply!'

On the opposing side, Mr Grant told his players to play the same counter-attacking game they had played in the first half. 'And keep an eye on Dermott Riley; he's been quiet in the first half. From what I've seen of him in this tournament, that won't last.'

It was a timely and shrewd warning. No sooner had they kicked off than Dermott took a roll-out from Dominic Jasinski, dummied past Dougie

Butt and dinked a crafty shot between the keeper's legs. It was the first time in the tournament that Yellow House had gone behind.

'Now we'll see what you're made of,' Mr Grant whispered under his breath. He didn't have to wait long. After one minute precisely, Duc Duong went on one of his lightning-fast runs, took a return pass from Albinus Gardiner and swerved the ball into the corner of the goal.

Seconds later, Blue House's Jack Mayhew took a roll-out from Dominic Jasinski, saw Luan Havolli gallop like greased lightning into a forward position, released the ball, and Luan crashed it into the net.

Once again Yellow House were a goal down. And then came the flukiest goal of the whole tournament. Dominic Jasinski rolled the ball to Dicky Woodward, who decided it was time to do his Ronaldo step-over routine. He glided past Albinus Gardiner and blasted a first-time, long-range shot towards the Yellows' goal. The crowd watched as it cannoned into the legs of Charlie Oakley and ricocheted back past Dominic into the Blue House goal. Charlie raised his hands to the sky. He couldn't believe it. It was the luckiest goal he had ever scored.

Three minutes to go and it was all square. The game swung from end to end and shots rained in on both goalkeepers. First Dominic tipped a vicious drive round the post from Albinus, and then Dougie Butt got his outstretched foot to a bending shot from Dermott Riley.

The seconds were ticking by, and both team managers were looking anxiously at their watches. Just before the final whistle, Duc Duong popped up five yards from goal with the ball and looked set to score before being robbed by Jack Mayhew, who quickly turned defence into attack. He nutmegged Albinus and rolled the ball into the goal. That was it.

Mr Mansell blew the final whistle and the Bridgewood High 5-a-side champions for the first time ever were Blue House. 'Blue is the colour, Blue is the name,' rang out from the Blue House spectators, as most of the players collapsed to the ground exhausted. It had been a non-stop, all-action final and it had taken its toll on all of the players.

Mr Cauldwell was delighted and was running round taking bottles of water to his players. None of the spectators had left their seats because all eyes were on the magnificent trophy, which glistened on a pedestal at the far end of the hall.

'Well, well, well,' gasped Mr Hyde, motioning for Mr Grant to follow him into the office. 'Nobody can say that wasn't a roaring success!'

'They certainly can't. I don't think there was a bad game in the whole competition. And that final! I think it deserves to be called a classic!'

'And how fitting that young Mr Mayhew should score the winner. What a turnaround in his fortunes since this tournament started.'

Mr Hyde gleefully rubbed his hands. 'Of course, he doesn't know the really good news yet, does he? Do we get him in here now or shall we make the presentations and then tell him?'

'I reckon we should make the presentations first. That way we can let the spectators go home and then get those that are involved to come in so we can explain what has happened.'

At that moment, Salam Chalabi knocked on the office door. He looked very upset.

'Sir, Sir,' he blurted out, his face wrinkled in a worried frown. 'I just went to the changing rooms to get my inhaler. My money's not in my pocket and my MP3 player has gone, too.'

'Sit down, Salam, and don't worry. Your money and your MP3 are safe. You'll find that when Jack Mayhew gets changed, he'll have your money and your MP3 in his pockets.'

Salam's jaw dropped. 'You mean Jack ...'

'No, he didn't. Jack never took your things. Somebody else did, but we will explain everything properly after the presentation. In the meantime, don't worry, all your possessions are safe.'

Mr Hyde ushered Salam back out onto the playing area, and he and Mr Grant left to gather all the players and move them down to where the trophy was waiting to be collected by Dominic Jasinski, captain of the Blues.

Everybody from the seated area moved down to where the trophy was. Everybody, that was, except Dan Pollard and Matthew Chapman, who skulked off in the other direction with smug expressions on their faces.

Charlie Oakley had seen them, and so had Jack Mayhew. 'See that, Jack? The bully-boys don't want to watch the presentation. I wonder why …?'

'Well, they don't like football. They don't like any sport. I don't know why they even bothered coming. Probably to scare me or put me off my game. That's the sort of thing they would do.'

Jack Mayhew watched them disappear out of sight.

'No mate, they had a bigger reason than that,' Charlie told him with a cheeky grin.

Jack tramped off, scratching his head, and Charlie and Mitzi joined him by the trophy. Mitzi couldn't stop giggling and telling everybody how excited she was.

The presentation was an inspirational affair, and when it was over all the finalists gloried over their medals ... except for Albinus, who was asking if anybody wanted to buy his. 'Any offers?' he was asking anybody who came near him. 'I'm skint! All contributions will go to the Albinus Gardiner Hamburger fund ...'

When the celebrations subsided, Mr Hyde asked Jack, Charlie, Mitzi, Salam and the PE teaching staff to come to the office. Once inside, he told everybody that the thefts would be solved in a few seconds. Mitzi took centre stage.

'You all know what happened with Hamit's money the other afternoon. This afternoon the same has happened, but this time the victim was Salam. The intended victim, however, was Jack Mayhew.'

Mitzi went on to describe how Pollard and Chapman had been at Jack's last school and had bullied pupils, including Jack, constantly.

'I want you to gather round. Mr Reece and I have some video footage that will suggest what happened the other day and show you exactly what happened this afternoon.'

Jack Mayhew's mouth hung open as Mitzi prepared to reveal what had actually taken place on that awful afternoon. The dark feelings of despair swept over him once more.

'Move closer. The following video footage was taken covertly by Mr Reece in the changing rooms during today's matches,' said Mitzi.

Everybody crowded round the small monitor and a buzz of curiosity and amazement filled the room.

The film footage showed Pollard coming into the changing rooms, creeping along to where the players' clothes were hung on pegs. He kept looking around him and seemed petrified.

'Right, now this is Pollard when he located the clothing he had seen Salam arrive in. Here he goes through Salam's pockets and pulls out the money and then the MP3 player. Now he looks around to find Jack's clothes. Look – he's seen them, and he creeps over and transfers the items to Jack's clothing. That's it. Job done. He sneaks out of the changing rooms and makes his way back to his seat next to Chapman,' said Mitzi, glowing with pride.

Gasps of disbelief filled the room. Mr Hyde walked over to Mitzi and she handed him a small black box.

'So as to leave nothing to chance, Mitzi used this highly sensitive recording device to tape Pollard and Chapman's conversations during the tournament. When I switch it on, you'll hear what the two culprits said to each other.'

The first voice was Chapman's. 'Done?'

Pollard answered. 'Sweet as.'

'What d'you get?'

'Some money and an MP3 player.'

'Cool. You sure you planted it on Mayhew?'

'Dead sure. It was the same clothes he wore when he came in here.'

'Well done, Dan. I can't wait 'til tomorrow. He'll be in big trouble.'

Mr Hyde switched off the recorder. 'Well done, Mitzi.'

Everybody echoed his sentiments and all attention focused on Jack Mayhew who looked to be in shock.

'Well, that's it, Jack. I don't think those two will be troubling you any more. There'll be an emergency meeting of the school governors in the morning, where we will decide what steps to take against Chapman and Pollard – but my bet is the police will be informed, the boys will receive a caution and we will exclude them from the school.'

'Can you imagine their faces when they find out that they've been sussed? I hope I'm there to see it!' Charlie Oakley couldn't stop laughing, and he gave Mitzi a big squeeze around her shoulders.

The trial matches
and bad outside influences

The governors' meeting took place, and Mr
Hyde's predictions were correct. Pollard and
Chapman were escorted off the school premises,
swearing and shouting, accompanied by a
policeman. Much to Charlie's annoyance, no
pupils were allowed near enough to see it.

Strangely, Jack Mayhew was deeply thoughtful
over the events of the past week. Charlie was
puzzled.

'Come on, Jack, cheer up. They're gone – and
good riddance. You ought to be doing a
celebration dance, not looking like all your hair's
fallen out.'

'I know, Charlie. The trouble is, they won't
leave it there.'

Charlie didn't think the two bullies would

target Jack again, but he could see that Jack wasn't so sure. Jack's shoulders were slumped, his head was low, and Charlie couldn't help thinking that his friend looked like an easy target for bullies.

Charlie gave Jack a friendly punch on the shoulder. Realising he had the support of friends like Charlie Oakley, Jack seemed to brighten up. Jack took a deep breath, pulled himself upright and even managed to give his new friend a weak smile.

What must it feel like to be strong enough to stand up to people like Pollard and Chapman? He looked at Charlie's solid frame and wished he was more like him. He told himself that he must go along when Charlie had his next fight at his boxing club. He couldn't see how anybody could beat Charlie Oakley. No wonder Mitzi thought the world of him.

In the aftermath of the dramatic events, it proved to be a bad day for the teaching staff at

Bridgewood High. The levels of concentration were at an all-time low. Everybody was talking about the 5-a-side tournament and the way Matthew Chapman and Dan Pollard had been caught out by Mitzi in their low-life schemes.

Mitzi Hasset was the talk of the school, and Jack Mayhew was in danger of developing a cult status: the last thing his shy nature would be able to deal with.

The English class that day was devoted to finding students who wanted to write for the school magazine. It turned into a brainstorming session with lots of ideas for articles being tossed about.

In Art and Design, Mr Redgrove was also occupied with the magazine. His task was to find students who would be capable of handling the graphics, with a little help from him.

He had a few candidates in mind, and heading that list was Angelo Paggio. Angelo had already indicated how much design interested him.

The other two possibilities were Salam Chalabi and Lauren Gooch. He had heard that Lauren was good at art, as well as being rather taken with Timothy Houghton-Smith. He was sure they would work well together.

By the time Mr Newlove's English lesson had finished, there were about ten students who wanted to be involved in the writing of the magazine, and Mr Redgrove had six definites for the design team.

Assured that the magazine was on course to get off the ground, Mr Redgrove was already allocating an area of his studio where Angelo's team could work. It was suggested that the editor and the art team should meet to agree the content of the first issue and decide the date it would be ready to be published.

Meanwhile, as expected, everybody who had played in the 5-a-sides wanted to play in the trials for the school team, and a lot more players besides.

Following the excellent individual and team performances in the 5-a-side tournament, Mr Grant and Mr Cauldwell had decided that Bridgewood High FC should play its first friendly against St Paul's Academy – the best team in East London. St Paul's were winners of Division One last season, and finalists in the London Schools Knockout Cup.

The other good news was that Mr Mansell had been appointed as Football Development Officer and would liaise between Bridgewood High FC and the academies in the area.

Some of the Bridgewood boys were already with academies. Charlie Oakley had been with West Ham since he was ten; Dicky Woodward has been on Charlton Athletic's books since he was eleven; Dominic Jasinski was on associate schoolboy forms with Dagenham and Redbridge; and Chelsea had shown interest in Angelo Paggio when he was at his last school.

Mr Mansell's job was to make sure that the

Bridgewood High FC players who showed enough ability – and had the ambition to progress – joined a suitable academy. Having watched the 5-a-side tournament, he thought that many of the pupils had a very rosy footballing future ahead of them.

Mr Mansell and Miss Cranson seemed to eat, sleep and drink football and, if rumours circulating among staff at Bridgewood High were to be believed, they would soon become Mr and Mrs Mansell – they seemed to be a perfect match.

Apart from playing for Dagenham and Redbridge, Mr Mansell was taking his UEFA Coaching Licence. Now he had accepted the role of Football Development Officer at Bridgewood, he and Miss Cranson would have even more footballing exploits in common.

Seventy students wanted to play in the trials. Mr Cauldwell realised the process of narrowing it down to just eleven players to represent the school was not going to be easy, especially as the game against St Paul's was only two weeks away.

'I had a feeling these boys were keen, but this is staggering. Everybody wants to be involved. It's great!' exclaimed Mr Cauldwell.

In the end, it was decided that there would be six teams with all three games being played at the same time. The trials would be on Friday afternoon, giving the players seven clear days before the big match. Once again, Bridgewood High was in the grip of football fever.

Everybody was looking forward to the match – although they knew St Paul's should win easily, there was always the hope that an upset was on the cards.

6

The trialists
show their class

Friday afternoon couldn't come quickly enough for the pupils due to play in the trials. It was fortunate, then, that Thursday was also a recruitment day – not for football, but for the Bridgewood High athletics team.

Miss Cranson was aware that she was clueless about the ability, in any events, of her new students.

She had heard on the grapevine that Aaron Jacobs ran a very swift 100 metres and that Jack Mayhew had shown no small amount of pole-vaulting ability, but apart from these two she was in the dark.

Once again, the teachers at Bridgewood High were astounded at the response. Thirty pupils showed up, and because there was so much interest, Miss Cranson promised she would book a day at the Crystal Palace Sports Centre. She planned to put everybody through their paces to get some idea of what talent they had in the school.

Timothy Houghton-Smith had decided he would give athletics a miss: his calendar was already packed full. Dougie Butt decided he would give it a miss because it was too much like hard work.

That was before they knew that Hannah Jardine and Lauren Gooch had put their names down for track and field events. Suddenly, Timothy expressed a great interest in doing the high jump, and Dougie let it be known that he threw a very mean discus.

Albinus Gardiner had recorded some promising times in the 1,500 metres event, but could not now remember why he had become involved in such a demanding activity. Unfortunately for him, Miss Cranson was soon told about his ability in this event, and was after him like a dog with a bone to get him to change his mind. Nobody doubted who would win the battle.

Sam Smith decided it would be a good idea to get involved. Not only was he a fitness fanatic, but why wouldn't anyone want to be involved in something Miss Cranson was taking? Sam agreed with Dominic Jasinski that Miss Cranson was gorgeous. 'How lucky is Mr Mansell to be marrying her?' Dominic had observed.

The football team trialists found that Friday morning in the classroom was its usual agony. The footballers were thinking of nothing but the games that afternoon. When the lunch bell rang, they grabbed their kit and headed for the coaches Mr Grant had arranged. The trials were on such a large scale that they were being held at the local sports centre, with its fantastic array of outdoor pitches.

The PE staff and Mr Mansell had picked the teams, concentrating on getting them as evenly matched as they could. The only form guide they had to go on was the 5-a-side tournament, but they were sure they had managed to pick teams that would make the afternoon competitive. After all, runaway victories were not going to give them the feedback they were looking for.

The captains were chosen and each proudly looked down his own team list.

'The Hamit Erbakan ll! How cool does that sound?' Hamit wasn't the only one to be pleased. Charlie Oakley, Dominic Jasinski, Jimmy Cork, Sam Smith and Johnny Cunningham were also chosen as team captains and all had smiles on their faces.

Mr Newlove came along in case any of the referees or linesmen was injured or, at least, that was what he said, confessing to Mr Grant that he wouldn't miss the trials for anything in the world. Mr Hyde was also surplus to requirements, but satisfied himself that he had left the school in the very capable hands of

Deputy Head, Mrs Howells.

The pitches looked splendid and would have graced any professional ground with their straight mowed patterns and close-cut grass. The line markings were newly laid and the goalposts and nets glistened in the shimmering afternoon sunlight. It was perfect weather for football, cold but crisp, with a very low wind.

'If you can't play on this, lads, you can't play,' said Mr Cauldwell, as he clapped his hands and called all the players around him.

He reminded them of his golden rule for playing good football. 'Remember, it's a sin to give the ball away if you can keep it.'

Mr Grant was sure there would be several players not in the provisional twenty-two who would come into the reckoning by the end of the afternoon.

Of the twenty-two 'Likely Lads', as Mr Cauldwell had christened them, Charlie's team had Ajit Kumble and Dicky Woodward in it.

Jimmy Cork's team had Luan Havolli, Duc Duong and Dermott Riley.

Charlie's team appeared to have been burdened with an overweight goalkeeper, who did not look as though agility was his strong point.

Mr Mansell, who was watching this game, thought it was a good thing that Ajit and Charlie, the two most capable defenders he had seen in the 5-a-side, were in front of Ryan Hartley, known at his old school as 'Podge'.

His prejudgment was soon to be proved wrong. Duc Duong went on one of his lightning raids down the right flank, managed to get past Ajit and unleashed a rasping shot towards the top left-hand corner of the goal. Podge moved across the goal line with remarkable agility and, with outstretched arm and totally horizontal body, managed to get his fingertips to the ball to turn it round for a corner.

'I've not seen a better save in the Premier League,' Mr Mansell whispered under his breath.

'Well done the keeper!' he shouted. When Ryan came out to claim the corner and threw the ball out accurately to a wide player in space, his admiration was complete. 'Where did he come from?' Mr Mansell said to Mr Newlove, who was going into raptures over Ryan's incredible save.

The game was evenly poised until a tall, skinny lad with a shock of fair hair dribbled the ball past three players, cutting in from the left flank, and slotted the ball past Jimmy Cork's keeper low into the net.

'And where did he come from? asked Mr Newlove. 'He didn't play in the Fives either, did he?'

'His name's Justin Cornard. He's fourteen,' said Mr Mansell, looking at his clipboard. 'You'd have thought, being that good with a ball, he would have wanted to play in the Fives, wouldn't you?'

'Perhaps there was a reason why he couldn't,'

Mr Newlove replied. 'Some of these kids have
tough lives. One lad in my form has to babysit
his sister five nights a week. He said she's
naughty and that's why he struggles with his
homework. The agonised way he told me about
it, I believe him. I asked him where his mother
was, and he said she has to work in the evenings
and doesn't get home 'til after twelve. He hasn't
seen his dad for five years.'

Duc Duong and Dermott Riley were starting to
run the game for Jimmy Cork's ll, and it was
only the stubborn defence of Charlie and Ajit,
plus another two fantastic saves from Ryan
Hartley, that kept the score in their favour by
the time the teams turned round at half-time.

Mr Grant was watching the game between
Hamit's ll and Dominic's ll. The two teams
looked as though they had listened intently to
Mr Cauldwell's message before the kick-off, with
a lot of prolonged possession being enjoyed by
both sides.

'I like that about some of the kids I've seen so far at this school,' said Mr Grant. 'They seem to appreciate that side of the game more than most kids I've worked with in the past.'

Salam Chalabi was giving a master display of midfield authority, breaking down opposition attacks with regularity, and spraying accurate passes to his teammates all over the pitch.

'I like that Chalabi boy,' Miss Cranson bubbled as she walked along the touchline. 'He's a solid tackler, but when he gets the ball he certainly knows how to use it. He's got what it takes to play at a high level, I'd say.'

Mr Grant nodded his assent as Dougie Butt was spotted by Salam on one of his forward runs, and the driven pass scythed into his feet like a well-guided missile. Dougie accelerated and went past two defenders as though they weren't there before slotting home a glorious goal. Dougie could not resist one of his trademark cartwheels in celebration.

Albinus Gardiner had been quiet up to the last fifteen minutes of the second half – until Peter Schirtzer, who had to play in goal (much to his disappointment) released a blazing half-volley from his penalty area. Albinus took it on his chest ten yards over the halfway line before letting it drop for a top foot trap, and then bent a thirty-yard shot past Dominic, which crashed home just beneath the bar.

'I can't believe what I'm seeing here, Miss Cranson. Everywhere there's quality. In defence, in the middle and up front. It's everywhere, or am I getting carried away?' said Mr Grant.

'No, you're not getting carried away. These are good players. I'd say we've got twenty-five players here who would walk into most school teams,' Miss Cranson replied.

Over on the other pitch, Mr Cauldwell was experiencing the same optimistic highs. He had heard a great deal about Sam Smith, but what he was seeing on the pitch surpassed all he had been told. Sam was so comfortable on the ball.

'This boy is good,' he swooned. 'Look at the class. He makes enough time to take their bootlaces out!'

The first half was a bit of a runaway for Sam Smith's team with Aaron Jacobs, Christopher Coggins and Timothy Houghton-Smith all having a brilliant game.

'Christopher Coggins is something else,' said Mr Cauldwell to Mr Hyde. 'Who does he remind you of?'

'David Bentley?'

'Funny that, because that's who he reminds Miss Cranson of. Mr Grant says he's another Garrincha, but I'm sure it's just the limp thing. Remarkable lad, though.

'Some of these kids who've had a rough start in life seem to come out of it with a lot of character, don't they? I mean, take Sam Smith – his mum died and his dad disappeared off the face of the earth, he was sent to a care home, and he has no idea where his brother and sister were sent. And look at him now!'

Nobody in the school knew it yet, but it had been a good week for Sam Smith.

Sam and his family had been living in Manchester when his mother died and his father disappeared. When he and his brother and sister were taken into care, Sam was just five years old.

By the time he was six, Sam had been adopted and was living with his new parents in Essex.

From that moment, he had no idea where his brother and sister were. As he got older, it became a mission to find them and, with the help of his adoptive parents, Sam was sure he was getting closer. His brother Ben would be seventeen now and his sister Isabella would be thirteen. If, like him, they had taken the surnames of their adoptive parents, it was never going to be easy.

Sam's dad, as he thought of him now, had read a missing persons item in a national newspaper not long ago. A lad of seventeen, from the Manchester area, was trying to trace his younger brother and sister who he had last seen ten years ago. His name was Ben and his surname used to be Brown. That was Sam's biological father's surname.

Sam's adoptive parents had made contact and were driving to Manchester at the weekend to see if they could establish whether or not the lad was Sam's brother. Sam was so excited. His mum and dad hoped he wouldn't be disappointed.

The second half of the Sam Smith ll v Johnny Cunningham ll was a very different game, with Jack Mayhew getting a grip of the midfield, Angelo Paggio deciding he was letting himself down and Ronnie Stenson showing the competitive edge that he had shown in the 5-a-side tournament.

Angelo scored from a penalty after being brought down in the box by Timothy Houghton-Smith, and Ronnie Stenson fastened onto a Jack Mayhew through ball to round the keeper and roll the ball into the net.

The whistle blew and the players trooped off to a well-earned shower. The staff came together in the canteen and, over steaming mugs of tea, discussed what they had seen and who they thought would be in the team to play St Paul's next Friday.

7

The phoenix rises

Monday was a sad day in the week leading up to the game against St Paul's. It was the anniversary that everybody in the Lucas family wanted to forget – three years to the day that poor Harry's life had been smashed to smithereens by a hit-and-run driver.

An eyewitness said Harry never stood a chance as the speeding car knocked him down on a crossing, then veered across the road, scraping along a red brick wall before roaring off and leaving Harry a crumpled, bleeding, stationary figure on the crossing.

The eyewitness had been sure that a young lad drove the blue sports car and that another youngster was next to him in the passenger seat. He didn't think the driver was any older than sixteen, and the passenger looked younger than that.

Dermott Riley could vividly remember the terrible day that it happened. He and Harry's brother, George, were walking down the road where the accident took place, when George recognised the trainers poking out from underneath the red blanket that was draped over Harry's body. It was an image they still had nightmares over.

It was from that horrendous moment that George Lucas vowed he would find the driver of that car if it took him the rest of his life.

The police had sent circulars to every garage in the East End and Essex to report any sports car that came in for repairs and had signs of crashing into a brick wall. Not one sighting had been made.

George, his dad and Dermott had traipsed the streets of Docklands, where they lived, looking for the car and asking people if they had seen a blue sports car that looked as if it had been in an accident. They distributed leaflets to shops, pubs and cafés and had announcements made over the PA system at West Ham and Leyton Orient football games, all to no avail.

The accident had happened three years ago, and George's campaign carried on despite the break-up of his parents' marriage, which he was sure was due to Harry's accident. His mother had suffered a nervous breakdown, and the stress had badly affected his father. They were never the same again. George loved his dad, and the pain of not having him at home any more made him more determined to find the person who had ruined all their lives.

Albinus Gardiner lived near George and remembered the accident happening. His dad was a motor mechanic at a garage in Docklands, and he had contacted everybody he knew in the motor trade to keep a special eye open for the sports car.

Albinus didn't get enthusiastic about many things, but he passionately hoped George would find the person who had run down his brother.

Albinus confused his dad Courtney, who knew his son had a quick brain and would be capable of achieving whatever he wanted to if only he wasn't so lazy. Courtney felt guilty saying his son was lazy, but over the last ten years he hadn't found a more suitable word to describe him.

Albinus's mother, Mary, preferred to think he lacked motivation. At other times she was sure he lacked inspiration. Both his parents thought that when he started playing football, and found out he was very good at it, he would be overcome by enthusiasm. It didn't happen. He had the same attitude towards football as he did towards everything else: apathy.

Albinus had expressed an interest in cars when he had just turned thirteen, and Courtney had decided he would take him to the garage in the school holidays. Within a week, Albinus found out his interest stretched no further than seeing the cars of two West Ham superstars in the garage for repairs, and wondering whether he could get a ride in them.

Courtney was not a man to give up easily. He had suggested to his son that if he liked the thought of cruising in a luxury limo, why not become a professional footballer?

Albinus's reply had been a long-drawn-out 'Hmmm,' followed by an equally long-drawn-out, 'Might-be-a-good-idea.' It wasn't convincing enough for Courtney to tell Mary that their 'lazy' son was going to become a famous footballer.

That evening over tea, Courtney saw a side to his son that had rarely been seen before. Something had happened at the garage that really excited Albinus.

A sports car had been brought in for some work on crash repairs. The car looked as though it had not been used for years. Courtney had contacted the man who brought it in. It turned

out he'd bought the car recently from a local
scrap dealer.

Albinus was bursting with curiosity. He did
have the ability to get excited! His parents
were overjoyed.

'Go on, go on. Was it blue?'

'No. But somebody had done a crude brush job
on it and painted it black.'

'So it could be blue underneath?'

'It is blue underneath.'

'Yeah, man!' Albinus shrieked and whooped
like he never had before.

Courtney continued to tell Albinus that the
scrap dealer didn't have the logbook and had
sent off for it to be re-registered. 'When he gets
that back we'll know who owned it before it was
taken to the yard.'

'This is weird. Harry was knocked down this
day three years ago,' Albinus pointed out.

As much as he hated doing it, Courtney had
to curb his son's enthusiasm with a warning.

'We're not home and dry, son, even if we know who owned the car. It could have been stolen on the day of the accident.'

'Well, then it would have been reported stolen – and if it wasn't, it must have been the people who owned it that were in the accident.'

Albinus wanted to ring Dermott there and then to tell him the news. His dad thought it wiser to wait until the logbook came back. Albinus wasn't sure he could hold on to this one.

Earlier that day, Mr Mansell had opened the discussion on the three games at the trials. The first topic of conversation was the astounding game Ryan Hartley had for Charlie's team.

The staff were all enthusiastic. They were drawn by Ryan's bubbly character, smiling eyes and chubby cheeks. He gave the impression that he hadn't an enemy in the world, and probably never would.

Mr Grant thought Ryan might be the perfect understudy for Dominic Jasinski. Somebody suggested he might even push Dominic for the number one goalkeeper spot in the future, especially if his fitness improved with some regular training.

Justin Cornard had made a good impression and it was agreed he was one to look at once the season started. Miss Cranson made an important observation.

'When he was at Langford, Justin never really believed in himself. He's definitely grown in confidence since Peter Crouch started at Liverpool. Justin's tall and gangly, but once he saw Crouch playing for his favourite team, he realised he could play football too.'

Everybody loved Miss Cranson's story and there were smiles all round the table. They were all happy that two players had emerged from nowhere to be contenders for the squad, and it was reassuring that all of the 'Likely Lads' had come through with their reputations intact.

Mr Cauldwell singled out Sam Smith for

special praise. The other staff teased him as he used adjectives that wouldn't be out of place describing the best players in the world.

The next morning, Bridgewood High was buzzing with speculation on who would be in the team to face St Paul's.

Aaron Jacobs warned Mr Grant that some St Paul's boys he knew had been trying to find out who was in the Bridgewood High team. Mr Grant couldn't resist a wry smile, but commended Aaron on his sense of drama.

'It's true, Sir. They wanted me to find out for them. I told them where to go and they said they'd get someone else to do it. That's how serious they're taking this match.'

Mr Grant knew the St Paul's Head of PE, Mr Parker, from his old university days. He was certainly the most competitive man that he had ever met, and losing at anything turned him into a demon, but surely even Mr Parker wouldn't go to those lengths for a friendly.

Before the students for his gymnastics class arrived, Mr Grant had a lot of unopened mail to attend to. The first letter he opened told him just how much information had gone beyond the school boundaries. It was from the head of the West Ham Academy saying he would like to send one of his scouts to the match against St Paul's. The next letter was from Leyton Orient, and one more letter in the pile was from Charlton Athletic.

Meanwhile, in Mr Newlove's English lesson, the name for the school magazine was decided and a publishing date was agreed. It meant that Timothy Houghton-Smith knew his deadline.

The magazine's title was 'Phoenix': a metaphor for the creation of Bridgewood High, risen from the ashes of an old East End warehouse.

'So now, class, who knows what a metaphor is?' asked Mr Newlove. 'I suppose I better start with the editor of our illustrious magazine. Can you enlighten us, Timothy?'

'A metaphor, Sir, is a figure of speech. It's a representation. Phoenix comes from "like a phoenix rising from the ashes". This school didn't really rise from the ashes so it is a dramatic representation.'

'I couldn't have put it better myself, Timothy.'

Mr Newlove was happy with the amount of work the students were putting in to the magazine. Angelo had produced a dummy front page, which looked good enough to be on the stands at any high street newsagent.

Timothy was still short of people to write features for the magazine. Lauren had suggested they have a forum, and posted a notice on the main board in the school hall. Timothy wasn't surprised when only three people showed up. However, it turned out that all three had parents who were journalists. Samantha Goodyear's father was a features writer on a national newspaper and her ambition was to go on to university to study politics and journalism.

Samantha was a beautiful auburn-haired girl with fascinating blue eyes and skin like porcelain. Timothy was mesmerised and had to stop himself from staring at her.

Rebecca Goodenough's mother wrote for a national magazine, and Rebecca also had ambitions to become a journalist.

Timothy decided, there and then, that he must enlist the support of these two delightful young ladies, who he was sure would make a major contribution to the magazine.

He suggested that Samantha could be News Editor and Rebecca should be Features Editor.

The other student who attended the meeting was Nick Upton, whose dad worked for the BBC World Service and had covered many stories in Iraq and Afghanistan.

By the end of the meeting, Timothy felt he was close to having a good chance of putting together a readable magazine. He hoped he had the makings of a team good enough to go on publishing each month. As Lauren suggested, once the first issue came out, there should be lots of students who would want to contribute. They could even put adverts in the magazine asking for people to help out.

Lauren also pointed out that she had noticed how Timothy's eyes lit up every time he spoke to Samantha Goodyear; an observation that produced a red tinge in Timothy's cheeks and had him feebly denying that he was remotely interested in Samantha.

As the school day ended, Dermott Riley was walking towards the school gates when his mobile phone rang. It was George Lucas with great news. He and his brother were coming out of hospital before the game against St Paul's.

Dermott was bursting to tell George about Albinus's lead on the sports car in the garage, but he had sworn that he wouldn't say anything. He changed the subject to play it safe.

'When will you be able to play football,

George? We had the trials for the school team last Friday. Everybody from our old school was asking about you. Wait 'til I tell Jack you're coming back to school! He'll be over the moon.'

George didn't know for sure how long it would be before he could play football, but one doctor had said he would probably have to wait about six weeks. He also told Dermott that Harry was doing fine and already the graft had made a great improvement to the way his brother looked and felt. Harry's energy levels had shot up, and the brothers were both really happy. Dermott finished the call with a big smile on his face, full of hope for his best friend.

8

Big announcements

With only three days to go before the big game against St Paul's Academy, Mr Grant decided it would be a good idea to bring all his football staff together. They could pick the team for Friday and discuss how they would use the two training nights they had left.

Mr Cauldwell thought the most important thing was to develop the spirit that already existed between the players. He had noticed their attitude to the PE staff and each other, and thought it was a great foundation for Bridgewood High FC.

The PE teaching staff sat down round the table in the office with the notes they had made after last Friday's trials.

It was decided that Mr Cauldwell would pick the team but would listen to any further

recommendations from Mr Mansell and the
other teachers.

'Firstly, I want us to play a four-three-three
formation – but only because of the players I've
picked.' He tossed a piece of paper onto the
table, showing the names of the players he had
selected in the positions they would play.

Jasinski

Kumble	Oakley	Smith	Houghton-Smith
Chalabi		Erbakan	Gardiner
Paggio		Butt	Cunningham

Everybody else in the squad was named as a
substitute because it was a friendly.

Silence reigned as they surveyed Mr Cauldwell's
selections. A great deal of chin stroking took place
in the next few minutes before Mr Mansell spoke.

'One position concerns me: Timothy at left back. He tends to bomb forward whenever he sees an opening, and it might leave us open on that side of the pitch. Albinus doesn't like defensive responsibilities to get back for him.'

'I'd like to go four-two-four and have Coggins out on the left.' Miss Cranson played on the wing and she liked teams that played with two wide players.

'I like the team you've picked,' said Mr Grant as he nodded his approval.

'I thought about Luan taking the left back spot but I think Timothy is intelligent enough to understand his defensive duties,' said Mr Cauldwell. 'I also thought of switching the midfielders around so Salam is on the left, but he prefers playing on the right. As for going four-two-four, I think that's a bit risky against a team with so much attacking flair.'

'Point taken,' Miss Cranson said. 'I just love watching little Chrissy Coggins.'

They laughed, and it was agreed that the team Mr Cauldwell had picked would start the game against St Paul's. The team would be announced after training on Thursday evening. Mr Grant was tempted to post a team on the noticeboard that would be nothing like the team he was actually going to play, but decided that was taking gamesmanship too far. He wasn't prepared to sink to the same level as St Paul's Mr Parker – especially not over a friendly.

Training that afternoon went exactly to plan and was devoted to small-sided touch sessions. The players loved it because it meant they all got a lot of the ball and managed to weave some fascinating patterns. Duc Duong, Christopher Coggins, Angelo Paggio and Albinus Gardiner were in their element, and their movement and ball control brought out the best in the other players. Jack Mayhew had given Mr Cauldwell a few reminders that he should be on that team sheet and was too good to be left out.

The training session fostered just the sort of spirit Mr Cauldwell and Mr Mansell wanted to generate in the team. It made everybody eager for Friday's game, and increased confidence that they could get a result, even though the odds were heavily stacked against them.

After training, as Jack Mayhew was waiting outside the school gates for Dermott, he suddenly sensed that the light around him had been blocked. Looking up, he saw that he had been hemmed in by two burly figures. One looked about fifty and the other one about eighteen. They were both dressed in dark clothing and had woolly hats pulled down on their foreheads and over their ears. They looked angry and threatening. Jack felt petrified.

'You're Mayhew, aintcha? This is Mayhew, Kirk,' said the older one.

'Skinny little runt, aintcha?' said Kirk.

'You got my boy chucked out of this school, runt, didn't yer?' said the older one who, by now, Jack had guessed was Matthew Chapman's dad. 'The one that stabs people,' raced through Jack's mind.

Jack had just started to speak when Chapman's dad grabbed his blazer lapels and lifted him off the ground. The school railings crunched against his back and the stench of beery breath and cigarette smoke surrounded his nostrils.

'We fought we'd tell yer our Matthew is in a Young Offenders Institute 'cos of you. He got into mischief. 'Cos he had no school ter go to. Anyway, he sends 'is regards and wanted ter tell yer that when he gets out 'e's gonna pay you a little visit an' pay you back fer all you done fer 'im.'

Jack felt his lapels slacken and his feet return to the pavement, as his two brawny attackers let him go before swaggering off down the road.

Jack was shaking like a leaf when Dermott came through the gates to join him. He told Dermott what had happened.

'Bejabbers, Mayhew, why does everybody want to cause you trouble? You'd find a fight in a confessional box, you would,' said a shocked Dermott.

Dermott kept on talking as he and Jack headed off down the road. He wanted to boost Jack's spirits before they arrived at George's house. They were both excited about the visit, and Dermott was glad Jack had something else to focus on. George's mum welcomed them at the door and expressed delight at the flowers they'd bought for her. George was amazed and pleased by the news that Mr Cauldwell had reserved him a place in the elite squad of twenty-two, and was looking forward to attending the game on Friday.

Dermott asked George's mum if Harry could come to watch. She promised to have a word with his doctor to see if it would be okay. By the time they left, Jack had stopped shaking, and had decided he wouldn't tell Charlie Oakley about the unsavoury incident until after the big match. He wondered how long Chapman had been put away for and what he'd done to be put there.

Meanwhile, Mr Grant had heard on the grapevine that St Paul's were laying on a couple of coaches to take spectators to Barkingside for the game on Friday. Two coachloads wasn't a lot of people, but it was more than Bridgewood High were going to have supporting them.

Mr Grant decided that the best way to get some support for the match was to tell Mr Hyde what St Paul's were doing. He had an inkling that the headmaster would not let the matter rest there.

Friday was a big day for another reason. It was the day Bridgewood High would know whether their application to be voted into the third division of the London School League had been successful.

The school had learned that if it achieved

league status, a sponsor would back the team for things like kit, travel and equipment. If they gained entry to the league, they would automatically gain entry to the London School Cup – an exciting prospect, as they could draw teams from all three divisions.

Mr Grant knew that if their application was delayed, they had every chance of losing the sponsor. With any luck they would know the outcome before the game against St Paul's.

If Bridgewood attained league status, there was a possibility that their sponsors would support a pre-season tournament to Amsterdam. Mr Grant had taken one of his previous school teams to the tournament and thought it would do the Bridgewood High players a lot of good. Teams from Cologne, Hamburg, Antwerp and Zurich, as well as from Amsterdam and Rotterdam, already had their names down, and most of the games would be played at Ajax and FC Alkamaar's grounds.

Mr Grant was pleased on yet another count. He had received two more applications to send scouts to the Friday game. Millwall and Crystal Palace would have representatives at the match.

Thankfully, by mid-morning Mr Hyde had okayed three coaches to go to Barkingside. Notes had been sent to all forms saying that pupils who wanted to go should book their seats in the entrance hall during lunchtime.

At twelve o'clock the news came through that the London School FA had cleared Bridgewood High FC's admission to Division Three and to the London School Cup Competition.

The PE staff and Mr Mansell met up in the office to savour the news and to finalise arrangements for the afternoon game.

The reality of being in the London School FA League struck everyone when the fixture list for the first season was posted on the sports hall noticeboard. To actually see the names of all the other teams focused the fact that Bridgewood High FC was definitely on its way.

Mr Cauldwell had asked his chosen players to come to the sports hall so the staff could check that they were all fit and well. There was considerable concern when Johnny Cunningham turned up with a large swelling around a very black eye.

'What happened to you, then? What's the other fellow look like?' Mr Grant asked Johnny.

'Sparring, last night. Caught an unlucky one. I was being a bit flash with one of the older boxers so I deserved it.' Johnny's cheek had swollen to the size of a table-tennis ball and seemed to obscure his vision.

'Are you going to be able to play? I mean, what's your vision like? Is it affected?' Mr Cauldwell sounded concerned.

'No, it's fine. It looks closed but I can see out of it. I did another two rounds after I copped this and he never got me again.'

Johnny could see that Mr Cauldwell was wondering if he ought to play, and that was the last thing he wanted.

Mr Cauldwell grabbed a ball and made towards the door. 'Come with me, Johnny.'

They walked out onto the pitch and the teacher started to move around with the ball before hitting passes into Johnny. Some were on the ground, some in the air, some slow, some quick. Johnny controlled all of them, and that was good enough for Mr Cauldwell, especially as he had fired most of them in on the side of the closed eye.

'You'll do. Nothing wrong with your reactions there. The only thing I'm concerned with is if you get another bang on it. Precious thing, your eyesight, and we don't want to take any chances. I just want the school doctor to have a look at it.'

Johnny's heart sank. He could see the school doctor saying he couldn't play even though there was little or no risk. 'I'm alright, Sir, honest. Doctors don't know about sport. You have to take chances.'

'This doctor does, Johnny. He's a prop for Northants rugby team. He'll have seen people playing with worse injuries than yours, don't you worry.'

Mr Cauldwell was already on the phone. When he put it down, he told Johnny the doctor would be there in half an hour. His decision would be final. It was an agonising wait for Johnny before the doctor arrived: a giant of a man and very young to be a doctor, Johnny thought. He examined Johnny's eye thoroughly and Mr Cauldwell told him about the fitness test.

'Okay. You can play, but ...' Johnny's spirits rose and fell in a matter of seconds, 'you must wear a protective mask.'

Johnny's spirits soared again. Not only could he play, he would look like John Terry. That was brilliant! Charlie Oakley did a little dance when he heard his mate had been given the green light to play.

The rest of the team all reported fit as Johnny was driven off to the doctor's surgery to have a mask fitted.

Everybody loved the school's new black-and-white strip and a mood of quiet confidence was building among the squad.

Mr Grant had e-mailed the team's potential sponsors, who were called Quest, with news of the team's league status and attached the fixture list for the first season. He was hoping Quest would reach a decision to sponsor the team before the lads boarded the coaches and went off to the match. Mr Grant had also asked if they would be willing to fund a pre-season tour to Holland.

Mr Hyde called by to confirm, once again, that Mrs Howells would be acting-head for the rest of the day. Mr Reece had managed to engineer a timetable that, strangely, did not have lessons on that particular Friday, and Mr Newlove had managed the same shrewd piece of planning.

Mr Grant did a last minute check to make sure that the kit was safely packed in the hold of the coach. The footballs for the pre-match kickabout were in their bags, the match ball was safely stowed in the bag with the linesmen's flags, the medical kit was packed and the water bottles were neatly stowed away in their containers.

'There's more to a football match than meets the eye, eh, Mr Cauldwell? And people think it's just a case of kicking a ball round a pitch,' Mr Grant said, as he cast a final eye over all the equipment he had packed. 'I think it's time to go. I'll just check my e-mails in case Quest have replied. Be great to announce before the game that the pre-season tour is all systems go, wouldn't it?'

'A BIG boost, I'd say,' Mr Cauldwell agreed. Mr Grant went into his e-mails and his expression told Mr Cauldwell that he had not received a reply.

As the Bridgewood team alighted the coach, the atmosphere was electric. Dermott, Aaron and Angelo were singing raucous songs and Dougie Butt had conjured a coin from behind Ajit Kumble's blazer lapel.

On the spectator coach, Lauren Gooch, Hannah Jardine, Samantha Goodyear and Rebecca Goodenough were messing about, enacting the joy they would feel if Bridgewood High FC won the game. They were all on a promise of being taken for a burger as a celebration.

'Ooh, wined and dined in style by our football stars. Does that make us WAGS?' Hannah joked. Everybody in the coach laughed.

When the coach pulled up at Barkingside Sports Centre the two spectator buses from St Paul's were already there, and their supporters were circulating around the dressing rooms. There was some good-natured booing when the Bridgewood High spectators got off the coach to stretch their legs and have a look around.

Mr Grant told the players to stay on the
bus for a little bit longer while he made one
last check on his e-mails. The bus fell silent until
Mr Grant's large clenched fist punched
the air. 'Game on, lads. We're on our way
to Amsterdam!'

An almighty cheer rang through the bus until
Mr Grant intervened. 'And there's more.
We can take the full squad of twenty-two!'

Another, even louder cheer rang out and the
players filed off the bus.

'Go straight to the dressing room – don't
hang around in the cold,' Mr Cauldwell
instructed his players.

He ushered them inside, not only to get them
out of the cold, but also because he didn't want
them standing around when the St Paul's team
got off their bus. He knew they were a big side
and had heard that they revelled in their
reputation as the best school side in East

London. Mr Cauldwell knew that any bunch of kids could easily be intimidated by that level of arrogance, but especially his lot, who had only recently come together as a team.

The PE staff filed off the coach and headed towards the dressing room. Before they got there, the St Paul's Academy team bus arrived. What Mr Cauldwell had been told about their size was correct. Some of the first players to get off the coach were enormous. Mr Cauldwell recognised the first player as Rushton Baynes, a big, stocky lad and an England U15 striker, who was on West Ham's books. He had scored a hat-trick in his first game for England against Italy U15s at White Hart Lane and he had scored eighteen goals for St Paul's this season, and ten goals for London Schoolboys.

'Oh well, Charlie Oakley and Sam Smith, fill your boots and the best of luck. A baptism of fire,' muttered Mr Cauldwell to himself.

The next player off was Wayne Mulroyd, who

was nearly as big as Rushton and had played for Northern Ireland U15s. He was on associate forms with Manchester United and it was speculated that he would join the club as an apprentice when he finished school.

Mr Cauldwell decided not to watch the rest of them getting off the bus. The confidence and self-assurance of the first two was enough to tell him his players had a battle on their hands that afternoon.

He had a niggling thought that he had dragged his team into something they weren't good enough to win yet. It crossed his mind that it would be disastrous to be humiliated. 'It could put the team back a year,' he worried to himself.

Such thoughts disappeared when he entered the Bridgewood High dressing room and felt the atmosphere among the players.

He took a good look at his two centre backs, who appeared to be in fine fettle.

Charlie was a picture of health and fit as a
fiddle. He was a handsome lad, and his square
jaw gave him an air of being invincible. Sam
Smith, too, presented an air of calm confidence
and determination. Johnny Cunningham was
in front of the mirror, admiring his mask
and pulling the most frightening faces he
could manage.

'Right, lads. Thirty minutes to kick-off. I want
us out there ten minutes before for a little kick-
around. Before that we will do a warm up here
in the dressing room – and I want you all
doing it properly. We're not having any pulled
muscles when the game kicks off. Don't forget,
when the game's over I don't want you diving
under the shower. We will do a full warm down
and then you can get cleaned up. The warm
down is just as important as the warm up.'

Mr Cauldwell thought there was no point
in telling his team what they were up against
and nothing to be gained by talking tactics.

There was one positive thing he wanted to tell them and that was the poor defensive record St Paul's had. 'They've scored a lot of goals, but they've let a lot in at the other end,' he told the team. 'What I'm saying is, let's play the game against their back four, not against their front four.

'Right. Have a great game, enjoy it. As you already know, Charlie is captain today. Vice captain is Sam Smith. Off you go.'

The cheer when Bridgewood High FC ran onto the pitch in their smart strip sounded like it had come from three times the number of spectators they had taken to the match.

'Ooh, don't they look lovely!' Hannah Jardine exclaimed in a theatrical voice. 'They look well fit!'

If the way the team looked was any measure of success, they had already won the game. The team grouped together between the penalty area and the halfway line. Mr Mansell ran out with a pile of black-and-white tracksuit tops, which they all put on, and Mr Cauldwell ran out to take the warm up.

When they were two minutes into their warm up, the St Paul's Academy team ran out onto the pitch. Their supporters cheered but could not match the Bridgewood High welcome in volume.

St Paul's yellow and blue kit had obviously seen better days. The girls were quick to observe that they were nowhere as smart as Bridgewood High – as though the match result was already a foregone conclusion because of that fact alone.

As Bridgewood High finished their warm up, a van drew alongside the pitch and a young lad wearing a black-and-white scarf got out. Jack and Dermott saw that it was George Lucas. The rear door of the van was opened and a wheelchair was slowly lowered down. It was Harry Lucas, and he too had a black-and-white scarf round his neck and a matching blanket over his legs.

Jack and Dermott shouted and waved. Dermott shouted over to the spectators, 'That's George Lucas and his little brother Harry.'

As though orchestrated by a conductor's baton, a chorus of cheers, whistles and clapping broke out. Everybody at Bridgewood High knew the story of George's courageous gift to his brother. It was clear to see that some of the girls had tears streaming down their cheeks and a flurry of white tissues conveyed the impact the arrival of the Lucas brothers had on the Bridgewood High crowd.

At that point, another unexpected spectator strolled on to the pitch perimeter. It was Albinus's father, Courtney.

On the other side of the ground, Mr Cauldwell and Mr Mansell observed six men in overcoats who they knew were the scouts from the professional football clubs.

Mr Mansell collected the tracksuit tops from the Bridgewood players, who went in a huddle close to the centre circle. They broke up when the referee whistled for Charlie Oakley and Rushton Baynes, as captains, to go to the centre circle, shake hands with the referee and toss for ends.

Charlie was a big lad, but Rushton Baynes towered above him. St Paul's won the toss and opted to stay at the end they were already in. Bridgewood High FC were about to kick off their first ever match as an 11-a-side team.

9

Let battle commence,
and a great day for George

Bridgewood High FC could not have had a greater shock than what took place straight from the kick-off. A pass from Dougie Butt to Angelo Paggio was intercepted by a St Paul's player, who laid it into midfield. The midfield player spread it wide, and an accurate cross was met by the head of Wayne Mulroyd. Dominic Jasinski had no chance as a screeching header rocketed past him and over the line.

Mr Grant looked across the pitch to see Mr Parker, the St Paul's PE teacher, punching his fist in a piston-like movement of triumph. Images of a rout flashed across his mind; to be beaten by Bernie Parker would be a bitter pill, let alone suffering a drubbing.

The Bridgewood High team were all over the

place and appeared to have forgotten everything that Mr Cauldwell had taught them. St Paul's were cutting through the Bridgewood defence like a knife through butter. Even when Bridgewood players did get the ball they gave it straight back to St Paul's, and every time St Paul's attacked they looked as though they were going to score.

The next goal was not long in coming. Timothy Houghton-Smith was up against a very tricky winger, who seemed to be turning him inside out. In frustration, Timothy launched into a tackle that felled the winger, who lay on the ground writhing. The referee awarded a free kick on the edge of the 18-yard box, and the wall the Bridgewood High defence erected looked as if a bus would get through it. Mr Cauldwell and Mr Mansell shouted in unison for the wall to tighten. Too late! A fearsome drive from Rushton Baynes went straight through the wall and past the unsighted Dominic Jasinski.

With only ten minutes played, Bridgewood High FC were two goals down and facing certain annihilation unless they got their act together.

The winger Timothy had fouled had to be taken off and substituted. Mr Parker replaced him with a midfielder, probably because his team were two goals up.

At that point there was a change in the shape of the game. Timothy started to exploit the space in front of him and went on a run down the left flank. He got to the edge of the 18-yard box and pulled a ball inside to Johnny Cunningham, who hit a first-time shot past the diving St Paul's goalkeeper. The mask had certainly inspired him.

The Bridgewood spectators leapt up and down in relief. George Lucas gave his brother Harry a big hug. It was against the run of the play, but it would do wonders for their confidence. Mr Grant was especially pleased that a tactical error by Mr Parker had contributed to the goal.

After the goal, Bridgewood High FC looked like a different team. Instead of treating the ball like a hot potato they were starting to string passes together, and St Paul's were seeing less and less of the ball. Charlie and Sam were winning challenges against Rushton Baynes and Wayne Mulroyd, and Salam and Hamit were winning everything in midfield.

When the half-time whistle went, it was the St Paul's team that were pleased to hear it. They trudged off as though they were one goal down instead of a goal up.

'That's more like it, Bridgewood. Now you look like a football team. More of the same in the second half! Timothy, go forward whenever you can. There's acres of room over your side now. They may change that in the second half, but if they don't, you exploit it. You've seen what happens when you get the game up on their back four. That's why they've let in so many goals,' shouted Mr Cauldwell.

The second half started exactly the way the first half had. Bridgewood High's defence went to sleep and allowed Rushton Baynes to get behind them and score his second goal.

'Why are we such slow starters? We go to sleep from the kick-off. I reckon Ajit was having a snooze when the St Paul's player went past him. Now we've got a mountain to climb.' Mr Cauldwell couldn't contain his exasperation. He wanted his team to lift their heads, not let them go down.

For ten minutes, most of the game was played in midfield, with neither keeper being asked to make a save. It was a rearguard action, and Bridgewood were finding it hard to cross the halfway line.

Gradually, though, Salam and Hamit began to win the midfield battle, and when Albinus was pushed forward by Salam, he went on one of his silky runs. The ball seemed to be glued to his feet. A little one-two with Dougie Butt, and he carried the ball into the box before slotting home a glorious individual effort.

Even Albinus looked delighted as he jogged back to the centre circle. The spectators were thrilled, and Harry was clapping so madly his wheelchair seemed to be dancing.

In the next five minutes, Johnny Cunningham went close with a header, but there was a clash of heads that saw the striker slump to the ground. Johnny got up after treatment, but seemed unsteady on his feet. This left Mr Cauldwell thinking the worst and praying that the lad hadn't done extra damage to his injured eye.

Angelo had got into his stride in the second half and was taking on the St Paul's full back and going past him.

In contrast, Johnny Cunningham was failing to control the ball and was giving away possession. Mr Cauldwell knew he had to take him off. He held fire as Angelo moved in on goal after a run that had taken him past two players.

Mr Cauldwell was concerned that St Paul's, egged on by Mr Parker, had become more aggressive. They seemed to sense that Bridgewood were getting on top. A reckless tackle on Angelo as he cut into the 18-yard box scythed him to the ground. Mr Cauldwell immediately saw the blood coming through Angelo's sock.

Angelo could not continue, and Mr Cauldwell thought that Johnny was struggling to see the ball properly. He decided on two substitutions, and sent on Christopher Coggins for Angelo and Jimmy Cork for Johnny.

It turned out that Johnny was suffering from double vision and Angelo needed stitches in his gashed leg. Mr Hyde would see no more of the action as he drove the two boys to hospital.

With a quarter of an hour to go, the girls on the touchline thought their fast food treat was in the balance until Hamit broke out of midfield with the ball and gave it to Christopher Coggins, who went on a mazy run, dummied past two defenders and put a ball on Dougie Butt's head, which he powered into the back of the net.

Straight from the kick-off, St Paul's went on the rampage. A three-pass move found their left-winger in possession. He crossed the ball, and a melée of defenders and attackers rose to contest it, including Dominic Jasinski. Charlie managed to head it out for a corner. Unfortunately, when the five players fell to the ground, Dominic was underneath them and had twisted his knee.

Despite treatment and the 'magic' spray, Dominic could not continue. Ryan Hartley was about to make his debut for Bridgewood High in a game that could not be more delicately poised. The nervousness among the PE staff was masked by words of encouragement for their overweight substitute.

Everybody from Bridgewood High breathed a sigh of relief when Ryan came out to claim the corner and set Bridgewood off on a counterattack. For five minutes, the game bounced backwards and forwards with chances at both ends.

Then disaster struck for Bridgewood High. A perfectly legitimate tackle by Sam Smith on Rushton Baynes, who rolled over and over, was adjudged by the referee to be a penalty. The decision seemed to offer an instant cure, and the big centre forward sprang to his feet.

It looked like a David and Goliath contest, with Rushton Baynes bouncing up and down ready to take the penalty, and the overweight figure of Ryan Hartley bouncing up and down in goal. Poor Podge looked more like a space-hopper than a finely tuned athlete, and he waved his arms about in panic.

Baynes stepped up and crashed his foot against the ball, which tore off goalwards. Time seemed frozen. The moment of impact came when Ryan's podgy fingers and horizontal body tipped the ball round the post for a corner.

Pandemonium broke out! The Bridgewood High players descended on the prostrate Ryan Hartley as he dragged himself to his feet, his chubby face beaming the sunniest smile in East London. On the touchline, a fiesta of jumping, cheering, whooping spectators celebrated the amazing save they had just witnessed, and George and Harry Lucas went mad with joy.

A patient referee ushered the players to restart the game and the Bridgewood defenders looked round hurriedly for the players they needed to mark for the corner.

There was another almighty roar as Ryan galloped off his line to claim the corner before it reached the host of players all pushing and shoving in the penalty area.

Ryan hoofed the ball upfield as hard as he could kick it and waved all the Bridgewood High players to move up behind it. The kick was collected by Jimmy Cork, who brought it down with a slick top-foot trap and moved it on to Christopher Coggins. Christopher beat his marker and saw Jimmy sprinting past him into the box. He poked the ball forward into Jimmy's path, and the striker side-footed it home into the corner of the goal.

A crescendo of sound erupted from the spectators and Bridgewood players as the final whistle sounded. It was an amazing Bridgewood High FC victory.

Back in the dressing room, the excitement was intense. The players could not believe they had just beaten the best team in the London School Football League Division One. Mr Cauldwell was having a job getting them to collect their thoughts and do their warm down.

Mr Grant, Mr Mansell and Mr Cauldwell were all in the dressing room offering their congratulations. An almighty cheer went up from the players when George and Harry Lucas came in to congratulate them.

George crossed straight to where Albinus was standing and indicated to Dermott and Jack that they should join him.

'Albinus's dad has just told me some fantastic news. The sports car that knocked Harry down belonged to the Chapmans! The police think their eldest son, Kirk, was driving it and that Matthew Chapman was in the passenger seat. The police are on their way to arrest them now. They've told your dad that DNA samples taken from the car will prove who was driving,' said an elated George.

Jack Mayhew took a deep breath and felt his body relax for the first time in ages. It didn't look as though the Chapman family would be troubling him for a long time to come.

Mr Hyde returned with the two wounded players. Much to Mr Cauldwell's relief, Johnny had recovered from his double vision and Angelo's leg had been stitched up, so both boys were able to go back on the coach.

What a day it had been for Bridgewood High FC and everybody connected to the football team. It was the greatest start they could have wished for. Now everybody at the school was looking forward to their first season in the London School Football League Division Three and the London School FA Knockout Cup. Not only that, the team had a trip to Holland to look forward to, playing in an international tournament against sides from Holland, Germany, Switzerland and Belgium.

And, at last, the torment was over for George Lucas and his family. George couldn't wait to ring his dad.

Follow the team online at
www.bridgewoodhighfc.com

Follow the team online and keep up to date
with the latest Bridgewood High FC action.
The fan site includes player profiles,
photographs, a player blog, league tables &
fixtures, free downloads, match reports, polls,
competitions, Bridgewood
High FC merchandise
& much more!

Bridgewood High FC

the struggle for success

Publishing date: **September** 2008

Follow the team online at
www.bridgewoodhighfc.com

Available from all good bookshops!

Publishing date: January 2009

Bridgewood High FC

on the march

AUTHOR PROFILE
DAVE SPURDENS

Dave Spurdens has worked as a sports writer and journalist for twenty-five years. He has written for magazines including *Football Kick*, *Football Monthly* and *Football Digest* and was a football correspondent for the *Sunday Telegraph*.

His published football-related books include *World Soccer Skills*, *Liverpool Football Club – The Inside Story*, *Wolves – Our Way*, *Norwich City – Our Way* and the children's novel *Rowton Road*, which has a BMX theme. He has written four additional books on BMX and was the editor of *BMX Racer & Freestyle* magazine.

In his early days, Dave played football for Crystal Palace youths and reserves and was player-coach for Maidstone United. He held the FA Full Badge coaching qualification and was an adjudicator of Preliminary Badge courses for the FA coaching department. Dave also worked for six years as a football coach in South and East London schools.